Words by Anna McQuinn • rson

ZEKi SLEEP TiGHT

Alanna Max

Zeki has been busy all day.

Now it is time to slow things down...

He sips a goodnight drink
of warm milk.

He soaks in smells
of dark forests
where all the owls
are sleeping.

Dreamy cream
is a caress
on his
soft skin.

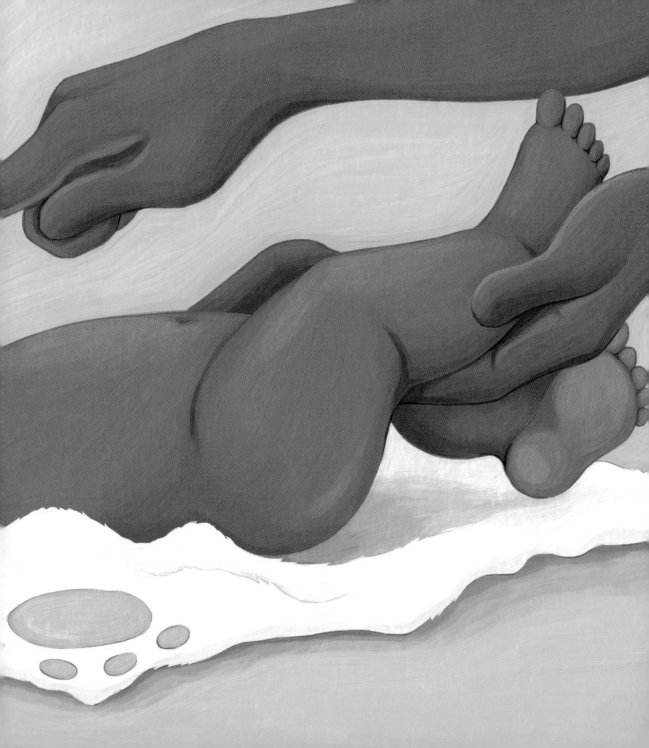

Zeki's fleecy sleep suit
is a snuggly hug.

With a swish,
it is dusk,
and the room
is hushed.

In the low light, they sing a slow song about a slumbering sloth.

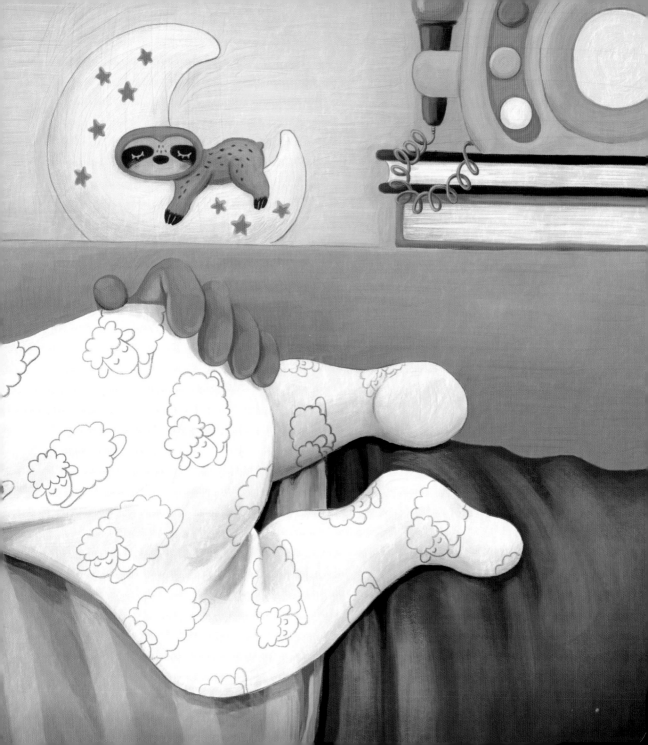

They read a dozy story
about a lazy cat
on a hazy afternoon

Zeki nestles
in his soft nest
ready to rest.

For Fay, for giving me the space to write
— A. McQ.

For Elodie
— R. H.

 Scan the QR code to visit the Activities
and Resources page on our website.

Published in the UK & Ireland by Alanna Max
38 Oakfield Road, London, N4 4NL
Zeki Sleep Tight © 2022 Alanna Max
Text © 2022 Anna McQuinn
Illustrations copyright © 2022 Ruth Hearson
Zeki Sleep Tight is part of the Zeki Books series developed
by and published under licence from Anna McQuinn
www.AnnaMcQuinn.com
All Rights Reserved
www.AlannaMax.com
Printed in China
ISBN 978-1-907825-44-6